THE HIPPO-NOT-AMUS

Tony and Jan Payne

illustrated by Guy Parker-Rees

GULLANE
CHILDREN'S BOOKS

Portly was a very young hippopotamus. He didn't ask
to be a hippopotamus – he was just born that way,
and he wasn't sure he wanted to be one forever.

THE HIPPO-NOT-AMUS

For Jason and Sebastien.
T.P. and J.P.
To lovely little James, welcome to the world.
G. P-R.

First published in 2003 in Great Britain by Gullane Children's Books
This paperback edition first published in 2004 by

Gullane Children's Books

an imprint of Alligator Books Ltd
Winchester House, 259-269 Old Marylebone Road,
London NW1 5XJ

3 5 7 9 10 8 6 4

Text © Tony and Jan Payne 2003
Illustrations © Guy Parker-Rees 2003

The right of Tony and Jan Payne and Guy Parker-Rees to be identified as the authors and illustrator of this work
has been asserted by them in accordance with the Copyright, Designs, and Patents Act, 1988.
A CIP record for this title is available from the British Library.

ISBN: 978-1-86233-514-1

Printed and bound in China

Hippos stood up to their eyes in water all day.
They ate boring old grass all day.
What sort of life was that?

One day Portly said to his Mum and Dad, "I've been a hippo for long enough, and now I want to be something else."
"Impossible!" said his Dad, shaking his head.
"You're a hippopotamus and that's the way it is," said his Mum.

But Portly was a very stubborn hippo. "We'll see about that!" he said, and stomped off. "It's time for me to be something more interesting and to eat stuff with a bit of taste!" he called back.

Portly had not gone far when he met a herd of animals.
More hippos, he thought. But as he got closer, he saw
that they had big spikes where their noses should be!
*You could do a lot of, umm . . . well, tossing stuff about
with spikes like that*, he thought.

"'Scuse me," Portly said politely to the nearest animal. "What sort of person are you?"

"I'm a rhinoceros," said the animal through a mouthful of twigs.

"Well, I'm going to be a rhino . . . thingy, too!" said Portly. "But first I need some spikes! Where did you get yours?"

The rhinoceros laughed. "You could
say I got my *horns* from my mother."
"Does she have any more?" asked Portly.
"No," said the rhino. "You have to grow your own."
"We'll see about that!" said the little hippo.

Portly found two pieces
of wood and sharpened
them until they were
pointed, like horns.

He tied them
on his nose, but
then couldn't see
properly.

He tied them to the sides
of his head. He tied them
on top of his head. He tied
them underneath his chin.
They just didn't look right!

He turned around to ask for some advice, but the rhinos had gone! So Portly carried on his journey with the horns sticking out just anywhere.

Before long, Portly saw a strange animal hanging upside down in a tree. That looked fun!

"Scuse me," he said. "What sort of person are you?"

"I'm a bat, I think," said the creature. "And you are?"

"I'm a **hippo . . . noceros**, actually," said Portly.

"So what do bats do, then?"

The bat took
ages to answer.
"Eat stuff . . .
hang out . . .
not easy being
a bat," he added.
"We'll see about
that!" said Portly.

He made some hooks out of bananas and tied them to his feet. Carefully, he climbed into the tree and then hung upside down. "Now what?" he asked. "Now," said the bat, "we wait." "For what?" Portly wanted to know.

The bat thought hard. "Wednesday!" he said. So Portly settled down to wait for Wednesday.

But after five minutes the bananas slipped and he fell out of the tree! That's when Portly decided that five minutes was just about the right amount of time to be a bat.

A little later Portly found a
waterhole. Standing in it
was an ENORMOUS animal.
"Scuse me," Portly said.
"What sort of person are you?"
"I am an elephant," said the
animal. "What, may I ask, are you?"

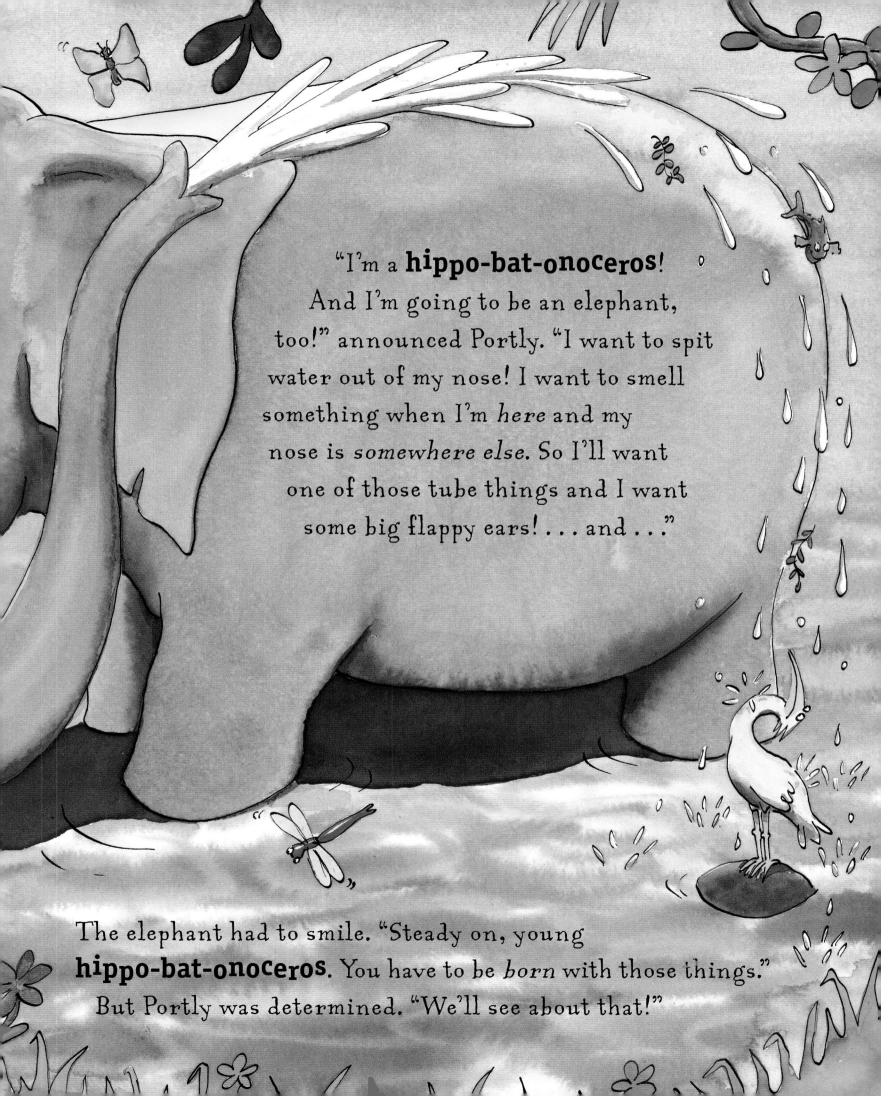

"I'm a **hippo-bat-onoceros**!
And I'm going to be an elephant,
too!" announced Portly. "I want to spit
water out of my nose! I want to smell
something when I'm *here* and my
nose is *somewhere else.* So I'll want
one of those tube things and I want
some big flappy ears! . . . and . . ."

The elephant had to smile. "Steady on, young
hippo-bat-onoceros. You have to be *born* with those things."
But Portly was determined. "We'll see about that!"

Portly made big ears from two large leaves.
Then he made a trunk out of a vine, but what
could he do with it? He wanted to trumpet
tunes and pluck leaves and spit with it!
And he couldn't.

So Portly decided to find someone else he could be.

His journey was slow because his horns fell over his eyes.
His hooks caught in bushes.

He kept tripping over his trunk.

And his ears flapped about
all over the place.

By now, Portly was
getting a bit bored
with excitement!
He kept thinking
about water, for
some reason.

Portly had not gone far when he met some new animals. They started on the ground, like you and me, but ended up above the trees!

"Scuse me," said Portly to a knobbly knee. "What sort of person are you?"

A head appeared from the leaves.

"I'm a giraffe," it said.

"What do giraffes do?" called the little hippo.

"Eat trees, mainly!" said the giraffe.

"Can **hippo-ele-bat-onoceroses** eat trees?" Portly inquired.

"I should think **hippo-ele-bat-onoceroses** could eat *anything*," replied the giraffe.

"Then I'll be a giraffe!" said Portly.

"But it takes years to grow all the way up here!" exclaimed the giraffe.

"We'll see about that!" said Portly.

Portly made two tall stilts out of branches and strapped them to his legs. But it was hard being so high up.

Portly was now hot and as hungry as a hippo can be. *I know just what I need!* he thought. And Portly started out on the long trail that led back to the river.

Portly's Mum and Dad were standing up to their eyes in water when they saw their son.

"Excuse me," said Mum, knowing who it was but not letting on. "What sort of person are you?"

"I'm a **hippo-gir-ele-bat-onoceros**!" Portly said proudly.

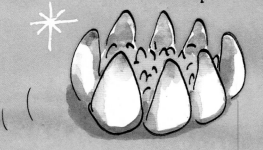

"Well, are you hungry?" asked Mum kindly. "I'm afraid we only have boring old grass for supper. Do **hippo-gir-ele-bat-onoceroses** eat boring old grass?"

"As a matter of fact," said Portly, "they like it more than anything."

"Then come and join us!" said Dad.

So the young
hippopotamus
removed his stilts
and slid into
the river.
The water felt
wonderful and
the boring old grass
tasted better than ever.
He did not notice his ears float away,
his trunk sinking and his hooks
and horns falling off.

Mum smiled at Portly, "Our own little hippo doesn't want to be a hippo any more, so there's plenty of room for you, if you'd like to stay?"

"Hmmm," said Portly, looking up at some nearby monkeys and wondering what it would be like to swing from tree to tree by his tail . . .

"We'll see about that!"